King Arthur and the Knights of the Round Table

King Arthur and the Knights of the Round Table

by
Sir Thomas Malory

Adapted by
C. Louise March

Illustrated by
Julia Lundman

Modern Publishing
A Division of Unisystems, Inc.
New York, New York 10022

Series UPC: 39305

Cover art by Julia Lundman

Contents

Part III: The Holy Grail

Part I
The Making of
a King

CHAPTER 1
WHO WILL RESTORE PEACE?

The marvelous tales that are about to be told took place long ago. Kings and queens lived in castles, and mighty knights and beautiful ladies filled their courts. When they were not at war, the knights competed with one another to see who among them was strongest and bravest. There were bitter rivalries and much confusion spreading through the land. People wondered if Britain could ever be united and brought to peace.

Vortigern, an ineffective and brutal king who had seized the throne, ruled the country. Eventually, Aurelius Ambrosius, the rightful ruler, aided by his brother Uther, dethroned Vortigern.

Then King Aurelius and his forces defeated the Saxons, who had invaded Britain and presented a constant source of danger.

When Aurelius died, Uther succeeded him to the throne. Uther Pendragon, as he was known, was a brave and mighty warrior. He preferred to be off fighting than at home ruling. For many years, King Uther had been at war with Gorlois, the duke of Tintegal in Cornwall. When Uther heard about the duke's beautiful wife, Lady Igraine, he called a truce and invited the duke and Lady Igraine to a feast at his court in London at Westminster.

During the feast, the king decided that he was in love with Lady Igraine. Later, when the king approached her, she refused him. King Uther was very angry, especially when he discovered that the duke and his wife had left his court without a word. King Uther ordered Gorlois back to the court. But the duke defied his orders. Outraged, Uther prepared to attack the duke.

Meanwhile, Gorlois left Igraine at their castle at Tintegal, a well-defended stronghold. He went to Terrabil Castle, hoping that Uther's men would follow him and not endanger Igraine. Uther took his men to Terrabil. The battle raged on both sides with many casualties, but neither the king nor the duke could claim victory.

Weary and brokenhearted—for he

had fallen deeply in love with Igraine—
Uther became ill. One of his confidants,
Sir Ulfius, went to find the powerful
wizard Merlin, who he hoped could
cure the king.

Ulfius had not gone far when a beggar
approached and questioned him about
his journey. Disgusted by the sight of
the beggar, Ulfius ignored him. But the
beggar would not go away.

"I am the one you seek," the beggar
said. "I will tell you what you must do.

Go back to the king with this message. I, Merlin, will make Igraine his wife if he will give me what I ask." When Ulfius arrived back in London, he delivered Merlin's message to Uther.

"Your love for the beautiful Igraine haunts you, King Uther." Merlin's voice echoed through the king's chamber, as if to punctuate Ulfius's message. Then the wizard himself appeared. "I will grant your heart's desire, King Uther. You will have Igraine, and you will

father a child by her. But you must do as I ask if this is to be," Merlin said.

King Uther eagerly agreed. Merlin said, "Tonight you will go to Igraine. With my magic, she will believe that you are the duke. Sir Ulfius and I will join you, perceived by all to be two of the duke's knights. Tell Igraine that you are ill and must go to bed. Remain in bed until early morning, when I will come to call."

Merlin's plan worked. Mistaking King Uther for her husband, Igraine spent the night with him and conceived a child. Later she learned that her husband was already dead at the hour Uther was with her. Gorlois saw Uther leave Terrabil. He decided to lead his men out to attack Uther's men. Gorlois died in combat.

Now that the duke was dead, King Uther's counselors advised him to make peace with Igraine. Ulfius went to Tintegal to negotiate with Igraine, who was eager to make a settlement. The

duke had been an elderly man. Although Igraine was dutiful to him, she had not loved him. King Uther's advances became more acceptable to her and, not long after Ulfius's visit, she agreed to marry Uther.

Two of Igraine's sisters were wed on the same day. Margawse married King Lot of Lothian and Orkney, while Elaine married King Nentres of Garlot. Igraine's youngest daughter, Morgan le Fay, was sent to a convent. Later,

Morgan would marry King Uryens.

Soon after the wedding, Uther noticed that Igraine was to give birth. He asked her about the child, and she told him about the man who came to her disguised as the duke. King Uther revealed that he was the father of the child. Igraine was very happy. She did not know about King Uther's agreement with Merlin.

But Merlin had not forgotten. He came to Westminster to get the child. "This child's birth will herald a new era in the land," Merlin announced. "He will be baptized and then he will go to foster parents until it is time for his reign to begin. I have chosen Sir Ector, who is a steadfast and noble subject. He and his wife will raise the child. We will not tell Sir Ector more than he needs to know. The child's origins will remain a secret."

Sir Ector came to the castle and agreed to the plan. He and his wife had one son, Kay, who was five years old.

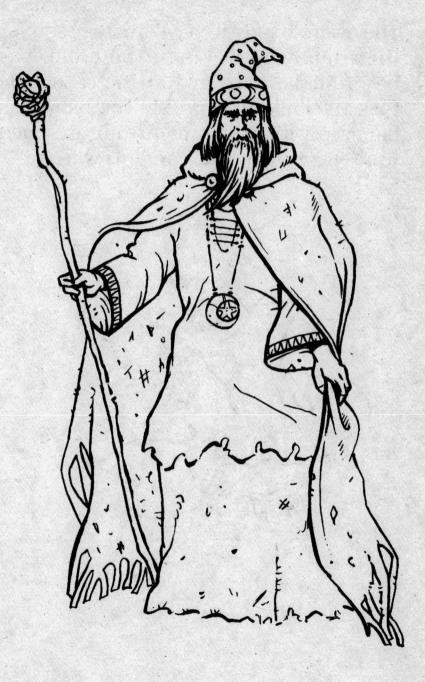

They were happy to have another son for their household. When the child was born, Merlin appeared at the castle. He took the child to a priest. The baby was baptized with the name Arthur and then was left with Sir Ector and his wife.

CHAPTER 2
A Boy Becomes a King

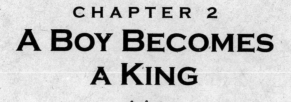

Arthur was not quite two years old when King Uther became gravely ill. The kingdom fell into chaos, with the king's enemies all vying for power and weakening the king's position throughout the land. Merlin told Uther that he must go to the battlefield. So the king was carried to St. Albans, where his army was fighting invaders from the north.

As Merlin had predicted, the king's presence rallied the royal forces. They defeated the invaders. Uther returned to London. The court celebrated the king's victory, but the king grew more ill. When it became clear that Uther would

soon die, Merlin called the nobles to a meeting in the king's bedchamber. With all of the nobles as witnesses, Merlin asked, "King Uther, will your son succeed you as king of all of Britain?"

The king struggled to speak. At last he said, "With God's and my blessing, my son will be king." Then he died. The next day he was buried and mourned throughout the kingdom.

While Merlin had made sure that the nobles understood the king's wishes, there were among them men of much ambition who desired the throne. For a long time afterward, the land was torn by war, and all of Britain was at stake. While this was happening, Merlin's plan continued to unravel.

As Christmas approached one year, Merlin told the Archbishop of Canterbury to call the nobles to meet in London on Christmas morning. On that day, a large gathering assembled at St. Paul's, the city's greatest church. When the archbishop announced that the true successor to the throne would soon be revealed, many of the nobles bowed their heads, secretly hoping that they would be the one.

As the noblemen filed out of the church, they saw that a block of marble had appeared in the center of the churchyard. A steel anvil sat on top of the block, and out of the anvil, a sword rose mightily into the air. Gilded letters on the anvil's surface drew the men's attention. The inscription read:

THE ONE WHO PULLS THIS
SWORD OUT OF THE STONE IS
THE RIGHTFUL RULER OF ALL
OF BRITAIN.

After recovering from their astonishment, many of the noblemen lined up to
take their turn, but none could pull the
sword out of the marble block. Since
they were all eager to prove their right to
the throne, a tournament was called for
New Year's Day. Some knights were left
behind to guard the sword. The noblemen left with their heads full of stories
of how they would triumph over the
others at the tournament.

News of the tournament traveled
quickly. Noblemen from estates near
London all flocked to the city, including
Sir Ector, who brought his two sons. Kay
was now twenty years old. He had
recently been knighted. He was looking

for a chance to prove himself to the other knights. Arthur was fifteen. He had no thoughts of fighting, but he was happy to accompany his father and brother to London, which he had never seen.

On New Year's Day, London was in a whirl of activity. Early in the morning, Sir Ector and his sons left the inn where they were staying. Arthur was told to carry his brother's sword. When they arrived at the tournament, Sir Kay discovered that, distracted by all of the

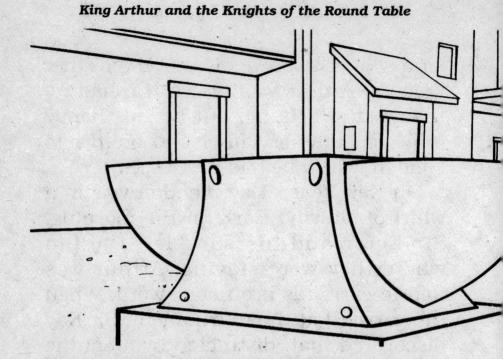

excitement, Arthur had forgotten the sword. Kay was very angry.

In a flash, Arthur ran off to the inn to get the sword. But he found that the innkeeper had gone to the tournament. The inn was locked. Even at so young an age, Arthur was smart and resourceful. He remembered seeing a sword in the block of marble on the previous day when he had passed St. Paul's on the way to the inn.

He dashed off and quickly reached

the church. Luckily, the knights who were guarding the sword could not bear to miss the tournament and had left their posts.

Arthur noticed the gilded letters, but he was in too much of a hurry to read the inscription. He grabbed the sword. It came easily out of the marble block. Smiling with relief, he ran back to the tournament to give the sword to his brother.

Kay recognized the sword, for it was

all that the other knights talked about. When Arthur placed the sword in his hand, Kay believed that it was a sign that he was to be the next king. When he told his father, though, Sir Ector shook his head. "You must pull this sword from the stone yourself," he said to Kay.

Sir Ector took his sons back to St. Paul's. He told Arthur to put the sword back in the stone. Then he directed Kay to pull it out. But Kay could not. Sir Ector was puzzled. He tried to pull the sword out, but it would not budge. Without a word, he pointed at the sword and looked at Arthur. The boy extended his arm. With a light grasp on the sword's handle, Arthur drew out the sword.

While Sir Ector did not know the whole story of Arthur's destiny, Merlin had told him enough so that now he understood why Arthur could draw the sword when no other man could. He pledged his allegiance to the boy.

"If you say this is true," Arthur said, "then I promise to fulfill my duty to this land and its people. You have been a kind and wise father to me. Anything you wish will be granted."

Sir Ector requested that Arthur make Kay his steward. Arthur agreed, and then they set off for St. Paul's to tell the archbishop what had occurred.

When the nobles were called to seal the succession, they refused to believe that Arthur was the future king. Some argued that he was merely a boy. Others said that he was not from the royal lineage. And one pointed out that it had not been proven that Arthur was the baby that Merlin took from King Uther's castle or that King Uther was the baby's father.

So another tournament was called for Candlemas. When no one but Arthur could draw out the sword on that day, yet another tournament was called for Easter. Again, Arthur was the only one to draw out the sword.

Finally, a few weeks later at Pentecost, Arthur was acknowledged by all to be the true king and protector of Britain. The nobles pledged their allegiance to Arthur, but some had grown to hate him and secretly planned revenge.

CHAPTER 3
KING AT LAST

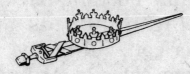

Arthur had a lot to do during his first year as king. Establishing peace in a war-torn country was his main task, but he also had to appoint counselors and form a court.

The year passed quickly. When it was nearly Pentecost, the anniversary of Arthur's coronation, the new king decided to turn his attention to his fiercest enemies, who resided in Wales, to the north and west.

He rode west with his counselors and knights to a castle at Caerleon, which is on the River Usk. When they arrived, he called for a tournament to celebrate the Feast of Pentecost and the anniversary of his coronation.

Reports from the country outside of Caerleon came flooding back. Six kings were leading hundreds of knights toward Caerleon. All of the kings had pledged themselves to Arthur's service, so he was not worried. In fact, he sent the kings gifts.

Meanwhile, Arthur continued to plan the celebration. Soon, his messengers returned with the gifts. They told Arthur that the kings had refused the gifts and were marching to Caerleon to attack! So Arthur took hundreds of his own knights to a tower stronghold and prepared for a long battle.

The battle raged on both sides, but the rebellious kings and their forces were weakening, and there was no sign that Arthur could be defeated. On the fifteenth day of the siege, Merlin appeared to the kings. "Tell us why this boy cannot be beaten," one of the kings said to Merlin.

Merlin told them the story of how Arthur was conceived. He warned them that if they defied Arthur, they would suffer. Arthur's destiny was sealed, he said, and nothing could change it.

None of them liked this answer, but they did agree to meet with Arthur. They were tired, and many of their own knights had gone over to Arthur's side. They hoped to buy some time in order to plan their next move.

Arthur, his chief counselors, the Archbishop of Canterbury and the kings and their counselors attended. Before leaving, Merlin had advised Arthur not to agree to any of the kings' demands. So the kings became more angry and left. Arthur took his forces back to their stronghold, and the fighting resumed.

Just when it seemed that Arthur's victory was assured, he was attacked from behind. Arthur fell from his horse. While some of his knights held off the attackers, Arthur felt for his sword— the one that had come from the stone.

Merlin had told Arthur not to use it unless his life was in danger.

Arthur sprang to his feet, showing off the sword. He cut down every enemy in his path and put an end to the siege. Triumphantly, he returned to his court, ready to vanquish all of his enemies throughout the country.

He called his advisers to meet. Merlin attended the meeting and told Arthur that the kings he defeated at Caerleon had found new supporters.

"You must make allies of King Ban of Benwick and King Bors of Gaul. Send your messengers to France at once to secure allegiance from these kings," Merlin said. "They need your help, for they are fighting King Claudas."

Arthur chose as messengers the trusted Sir Ulfius and Sir Brastius. Their journey to Benwick was not untroubled. They met and defeated a number of King Claudas' supporters. Finally, they arrived at Benwick.

Both King Ban and King Bors were at Benwick. They readily agreed to pledge themselves to Arthur's service. They gave Arthur's messengers gifts for the king and promised to travel to Britain to aid him.

Arthur graciously received Ban and Bors. He called for a feast and tournament in their honor. The next day, he met with them to plan the attack. Merlin traveled to France to assemble the forces of the two worthy kings. Two of Arthur's

bravest knights went with Merlin. They remained in France to help the two kings' followers fight King Claudas.

More than ten thousand men made the journey with Merlin from France to Britain. They arrived at Dover and then traveled to a forest at Bedegraine in the north. By the time that Merlin arrived back in London, Arthur had gathered together his own impressive number of men, including Sir Ector and Sir Kay. Together with Merlin, Ban, and Bors,

Arthur and his men went to Bedegraine Forest to prepare for the battle.

The rebel kings had led their forces—fifty thousand strong—close by Bedegraine Forest. As they approached the town, they attacked Bedegraine Castle, which was loyal to Arthur.

Merlin advised Arthur to keep his men under cover in the forest. With Merlin's advice, Arthur could attack with fewer men. His enemies, who would not know that more men were hidden, ready for an

ambush, would think Arthur was out-numbered.

That night, Arthur took his bravest knights and attacked the rebel camp. By the time the other kings realized what was happening, Arthur and his

men had killed or wounded many. When the fighting was over the next morning, the enemy forces were very seriously depleted.

Then, as Merlin had advised, Arthur took twenty thousand men into the open field to fight, leaving ten thousand in the forest. The rebel kings were delighted because they clearly outnumbered Arthur's forces, or so they thought. When the battle reached a fever pitch, Ban and Bors silently gave orders to the men in the forest.

The rebel kings knew that their men were exhausted. As they were trying to decide how to proceed, Ban and Bors charged with their men. It seemed as though Arthur could not lose.

Merlin knew better. As more and more men fell on both sides, Merlin told Arthur that he could not win this battle and instructed him to lead his men to safety. Arthur did not doubt Merlin's wisdom, but it is a hard thing for a knight to leave a battle unfinished. Merlin reassured Arthur that the rebel kings were no longer a threat. Since invaders had overtaken their own lands, Arthur's enemies would have to use their forces to keep their kingdoms intact.

CHAPTER 4
THE KING
PROVES HIMSELF

As Arthur's destiny unfolded, he had many adventures in which he proved his worth as a true steward of his country. Whenever one of his supporters was in danger, Arthur acted quickly to restore order and avenge wrongdoing.

A king from the west had attacked one of Arthur's friends, King Leodegrance. Leodegrance called for Arthur's help. At once, Arthur traveled with his forces to Leodegrance's castle at Cameliard in the southwest. With Arthur's help, King Leodegrance's kingdom was saved.

Leodegrance was deeply grateful to Arthur. He held a feast in Arthur's honor at which Arthur met Leodegrance's daughter, Guinevere. Her beauty and goodness captured Arthur's heart. Before the feast was over, Arthur had fallen in love with her.

Ban and Bors had traveled with Arthur to Cameliard. One of their messengers came to report that King Claudas had once again attacked their kingdoms. They had to leave Cameliard right away. Arthur insisted that he should go to France, too. But Ban and Bors could see that Arthur loved Guinevere. They urged him to stay in Britain.

Their counsel was wise, since Arthur was needed in Britain. The rebel kings had not forgotten the bloodshed at Bedegraine. King Lot, one of the rebels, felt that King Arthur would be a great ally in their struggles against invaders.

Lot was married to Margawse, Igraine's sister. Although the rebel kings were able to keep the invaders at bay by joining forces, Lot still planned to do something about Arthur.

With thoughts of the lovely Guinevere in his head, Arthur returned to Caerleon. Soon after, Margawse came to visit Arthur with her sons, Gawain, Gaheris, Agravaine and Gareth.

Arthur did not know that Margawse was his mother's sister, or that she was sent by Lot to spy on him. Perhaps because he was lonely for Guinevere, or perhaps because it was his destiny, Arthur became attached to Margawse. She conceived Arthur's son Mordred.

After this, Arthur's dreams were haunted by disaster. He could not shake his feelings of dread. Since he was restless, he thought that a hunt might divert his attention. A number of men went on the hunt. When they spied a white hare, Arthur took off after it and left the others behind.

Arthur rode so fast that his horse could not keep up. The poor beast fell down and died. Luckily, a forester passed by and told Arthur that he would search

for another horse. Arthur thanked him and sat down by a well to wait.

Arthur tried to quiet his mind. His thoughts continued to swirl, and the feeling of dread grew stronger. When he heard a loud noise, he leaped up. The sound came from a ferocious creature that moved toward the well. After drinking some water, the beast went back into the forest.

Fear and surprise caused Arthur to swoon. Whether he passed out or slept, he did not know. The only thing he could recall was being shaken by a knight he did not know.

The knight was, in fact, King Pellinore. He ruled over Listinoise. He told Arthur that he was chasing the Questing Beast. Since Arthur felt restless, he offered to chase the creature. At that moment, the forester came back with a horse. Pellinore agreed to let Arthur continue the quest for a year. Then Pellinore jumped on the horse and rode away.

Arthur felt angry and confused. He barely saw a young boy approaching. The boy asked Arthur about his great adventures. Arthur gave a brief reply and returned to his dark thoughts. But the boy did not leave. He told Arthur all that had just happened and how Arthur had become king. Arthur screamed at him, and the boy fled.

Then a wizened old man approached and asked, "Why are you so troubled, young man?"

Arthur told him about the boy. "I can tell you more than the child," the old man said. To Arthur's astonishment, the old man related how Margawse had tricked Arthur and conceived a child who would be Arthur's undoing.

"Merlin!" Arthur cried.

"Yes, it is Merlin. Come now, here is another horse," the old man said as the forester came out of the forest with another beast.

Arthur and Merlin rode back to Caerleon. Arthur's state was worse than

ever. Arthur called Sir Ector and Sir Ulfius to him to verify what he had heard from Merlin. The knights confirmed Merlin's words, but Arthur still refused to believe it. He wanted his mother, Igraine, to tell him what had happened.

So Igraine was called to Caerleon to tell her story. Ulfius demanded that she reveal everything to her son. Igraine pleaded with Ulfius for mercy.

"I do not know what happened to the

baby after Merlin took him away," Igraine insisted. She was very upset.

Arthur turned to Merlin, who repeated all that he had said about Uther and Igraine. Sir Ector gave his word that Merlin's words were true. With this news, Arthur's shoulders dropped a little, and he hung his head. Looking up again, he embraced Igraine and welcomed her as his mother.

CHAPTER 5
A NEW SWORD
FOR ARTHUR

Now that King Pellinore was no longer chasing the Questing Beast, he was causing a lot of trouble for knights who passed by his territory. Arthur heard about it and decided to put an end to Pellinore's tyranny.

One day, Pellinore attacked Sir Miles and killed him. Sir Miles's squire brought his master to Arthur's court, hoping that the king would avenge the death. A youth named Griflet approached Arthur and asked to be made a knight so that he could ride after Pellinore.

Now Griflet was not much younger than Arthur, but Arthur told him that he was too young to defeat Pellinore.

But Arthur did agree to make Griflet a knight, provided he stayed far away from Pellinore.

Griflet was overjoyed. He dressed in his armor, took a shield and a spear, and mounted a horse. He was ready for some knightly adventures. Little did he know that his first adventure would lead him straight to Pellinore.

Griflet rode by a fountain and was drawn to a rich pavilion close by. A horse stood outside the pavilion. A colorful shield hung from the branch of a tree, and a spear rested against the trunk.

The youth tapped the shield with his spear, and it fell to the ground. A mighty knight came out of the pavilion. When Griflet challenged him to a joust, the knight laughed.

"You are full of confidence, young knight," he said, "but you can't defeat me."

But Griflet persisted, so the knight agreed to joust. Poor Griflet was badly wounded. Pellinore put the boy back on his horse, and the beast carried him to the court. He was attended to by the king's healers and was made well.

When Arthur heard about Griflet's injuries, he was angry. He was in this mood when twelve knights from Rome came to the court to request a tribute for the emperor.

Arthur was furious, but he agreed to let the knights live as long as they returned to the emperor and delivered a message: If the emperor tried to exact another tribute, Arthur would defeat him.

Seething with anger, Arthur went off in search of Pellinore. On his way, he found Merlin riding through the forest. Merlin rode with Arthur to the pavilion.

"This deed you set out upon is a dark one," Merlin said, noting Arthur's anger.

Clouded by his anger, Arthur did not heed the warning. When he and Merlin arrived at the pavilion, Pellinore was seated outside. Arthur challenged Pellinore and they began to joust.

They came together three times. Arthur was thrown from his horse. He got up, raised his sword, and charged forward. Pellinore got down from his horse and battled until both kings were bloody and exhausted, but neither would give in. Finally, Arthur's sword broke. He was forced to tackle Pellinore and fight him by hand.

Pellinore proved to be stronger. He

managed to remove Arthur's helmet and raised his sword to cut Arthur's head off. If not for Merlin, Arthur would have died. Merlin cast a spell over Pellinore to make him sleep. This angered Arthur even more.

"This is Pellinore," Merlin said. "He is a good and worthy knight who will live to do great things for the realm. He will have two sons, Percival and Lamerak. Their names will be famous."

Merlin took Arthur to a dwelling in the forest where a hermit lived. The hermit treated Arthur's wounds. After three days, Arthur was well enough to travel, so he and Merlin left.

Arthur was sorry to have broken his sword, but Merlin assured him that an even greater sword would come into his possession. He led Arthur to a lake. A fine lady was crossing the lake in a small boat. In the middle of the lake, Arthur saw a hand rising out of the water. It held a mighty sword and a scabbard.

"That is the Lady of the Lake of Avalon," Merlin said. "She will give you the sword."

When the Lady of the Lake reached them, Arthur asked her for the sword.

"This mighty sword is Excalibur," she said. "In exchange for a gift, I will tell you what you must do to get the sword."

Arthur agreed, and she continued, "Row to the sword in this boat. Take the sword and the scabbard. When the

time comes, I will ask for the gift."

With Merlin at his side, Arthur rowed across the lake and took the sword and scabbard. As he did so, the arm that held them disappeared.

During the journey home, they passed Pellinore's pavilion. But Pellinore was off fighting another knight. Arthur was very disappointed because he wanted to try his new sword in a joust with Pellinore.

Merlin shook his head and repeated his warning. "Pellinore is the stronger

and he will defeat you." Merlin knew that Pellinore's destiny was to marry Arthur's sister, Acheflour. They would have two sons who would become knights of the Round Table: Percival and Lamerak.

Merlin saw that Arthur was extremely enchanted by his new sword and asked the king which weapon he preferred, the sword or the scabbard.

"The sword," Arthur answered, sure that he had given the right answer.

"Not so," Merlin said. "As long as you have the scabbard in battle, any wounds you receive will not bleed. Take care to wear it."

PART II
BRAVE KNIGHTS
AND
STRANGE
ADVENTURES

CHAPTER 1
BALIN SEEKS ARTHUR'S LOYALTY

It was good that King Arthur had Excalibur, since there still were many rivals plotting his downfall. But with Merlin to advise him and many brave knights willing to sacrifice their lives for him, Arthur was confident that he could defeat his opponents.

Arthur had not been back at his court for long when news came of another challenge to his authority. King Rience of West Britain sent a message to Arthur with a strange demand. Rience said that he was making a cloak from the beards of kings he had defeated. Now he required Arthur to contribute his beard to complete the cloak.

This message infuriated Arthur. He sent a reply stating that King Rience would soon be begging for mercy instead of a beard! Of course, a ruler as haughty as Rience refused to back down. He raised an army and planned to attack everything in his path until he reached Arthur's court.

Arthur called his knights together at Camelot to plan a counterattack. While the knights talked, a maiden came to the court seeking Arthur's assistance.

"The Lady of the Lake of Avalon sends a message to the king," the maiden said. Once she had the king's attention, she pulled aside her mantle and pointed to a sword and scabbard that hung from her girdle. "I am charged with bearing this sword until a true knight pulls it from the scabbard. Many knights have tried, but all have failed. None of King Rience's knights were able to relieve me of this burden."

"I will come to your aid," Arthur said.

But he could not pull the sword from the scabbard. He asked that all worthy knights at his court come forth to try. Afraid that they would prove themselves to be unworthy, the knights stayed where they were.

Arthur was ashamed of his knights. The maiden left the castle alone. In the garden, a man in ragged clothing approached her. This man was called Balin. He was a trustworthy knight, but he had been in prison for half a year for killing a cousin of the king during a joust. He had just been released and was eager to prove his worth to Arthur.

"If you will allow it, I will try my hand on the sword," Balin said.

The maiden looked doubtful, but she drew aside her mantle. The knight deftly drew the sword from the scabbard. Both he and the maiden were surprised at how easily it came out. When they looked up, they saw that the king and the other knights were standing around them, marveling that it was Balin who had been able to retrieve the sword.

The maiden thanked Balin and asked for the sword. Balin refused to give it to her. She warned him that if he used the sword, it would cause his death and the death of one he loved more than any other. Still, Balin was intent on keeping the sword. He planned to ride out in search of adventures that would regain the king's esteem.

Before Balin left, a fine lady arrived at the castle. It was the Lady of the Lake of Avalon. She had told Arthur how to acquire Excalibur. Now she had come to ask for the gift he had promised in return for the sword.

"I ask for the head of the knight who helped this maiden, or the maiden's head," she said.

Arthur shook his head. He could not murder Balin or the maiden.

"He killed my brother," the lady said,

"and she caused my father's death."

"I am sorry that you have lost your father and brother," Arthur said, "but I cannot do as you wish. Please ask for another gift."

Balin saw that the king was troubled by the lady's request. Since he wanted to prove his loyalty, he rushed forward and beheaded her. Arthur was shocked by this brutal act. He banished Balin from the court. So Balin left. He was determined to kill Arthur's archenemy, King Rience, and show Arthur that he was a true knight.

CHAPTER 2
BALIN'S FATE
UNFOLDS

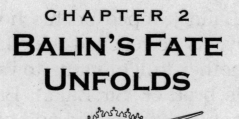

Balin rode out fearlessly. He had nothing else to lose but his life. One of Arthur's knights followed Balin. When he reached Balin, he said, "You must pay for the shame you have brought on our king's court. Prepare to battle."

Balin had little trouble defeating the knight, who was more forceful with his words than with his weapons. As Balin stood over the dead knight, a young noblewoman riding a horse came through the forest.

"When you slew this knight, you slew me," she said. Then she took the knight's sword and drove it into her chest.

Shaken by the bloodshed he had

caused, Balin jumped on his horse and rode away. As he reached the edge of the forest, another knight came toward him. It was his brother, Sir Balan. Balin told Balan what had happened and about his intention to kill King Rience. Balan agreed to assist him, and the brothers continued through the forest together.

They rode in silence until they saw a royal figure on a horse. It was King Mark of Cornwall, who at this time supported King Arthur. When he heard how the knight and the lady were killed, he rode off to find a tomb for a proper burial.

When King Mark returned, the two brothers began to dig a grave. At that moment, Merlin appeared. He said to Balin, "You have committed a terrible act by taking the sword from the maiden and causing these lovers' deaths. You will commit a more terrible act, still. With a single stroke you will cause three kingdoms to fall and will bestow an incurable wound on a noble king."

Balin hung his head. When he looked up, Merlin was gone. King Mark bid them farewell and rode off. Downcast by Merlin's prophecy, Balin was now more determined than ever to find King Rience now.

The brothers continued riding westward until evening fell. Then they rested until midnight, when they heard the sound of horses' hooves coming through the forest. King Rience and a company of more than fifty knights rode by.

Merlin appeared again. He told them

which knight was King Rience. Together, they brought down the king and sent his followers fleeing through the forest. Rience begged for mercy. Balin decided to let the king live. He wanted to deliver Rience alive to King Arthur.

Arthur rejoiced at Balin's victory, but he knew that another enemy was preparing to march against him. Rience's brother, King Nero, wanted revenge. So another battle raged, but Arthur was once again victorious.

Merlin knew that Rience and Nero had supporters. One was King Lot, who had married Arthur's mother's sister, Margawse. Lot was the father of four sons who would become Arthur's knights: Gawain, Gaheris, Agravine and Gareth. Lot had hated Arthur ever since his wife gave birth to Arthur's son.

Lot gathered all of the kings who had been defeated at Bedegraine and advanced on Arthur in Camelot. Both sides lost many knights, but finally

Pellinore killed Lot. Arthur was proud of his knights and wanted to reward them. He could not find Balin and asked Merlin where the knight was.

"Sir Balin has left your court forever," Merlin replied. "His fate is unraveling, and nothing can be done to change it."

CHAPTER 3

TWO PROPHECIES
ARE FULFILLED

Perhaps because he was troubled by the events that had caused Balin to leave the court, Arthur became ill. While he was resting in a meadow outside the castle, he saw a knight riding by. The anguished knight did not recognize the king. Arthur asked the knight why he was so upset. The knight just shook his head and continued on his way.

Then Balin rode by the meadow. Arthur asked Balin to go after the knight and find out what had happened to him. Before long, Balin found the knight in the forest. He was with a young noblewoman. Balin convinced the knight to come back to the court. They left the lady in the forest and returned to Arthur's castle.

To Balin's and Arthur's horror, as the knight approached the king he was pierced by a sword. But there was no arm or body attached to the sword!

The knight fell from his horse. As he lay dying, he gasped, "My name is Herlews le Berbeus. The invisible knight who slew me is Sir Garlon. You must go to my lady in the forest and tell her what happened. Then you must avenge my death."

Balin did as the knight requested. Together, Balin and the lady set off to look for Garlon. They met another knight, who offered to go with them. The group traveled for a while in peace, but when they reached a hermitage, they saw the sword carried by the invisible knight, Garlon. Balin and the lady cried out when the sword pierced their companion.

Leaving the body to be buried by a holy man who lived in the hermitage,

Balin and the lady left to follow the evil Garlon. A grand castle came into view, and Balin directed their horses toward it. When they passed through the gate, a number of knights grabbed the lady. Balin raced forward to defend her.

One of the knights held up his hand. "We mean no harm," the knight said. "Our mistress is under an evil enchantment. She is very ill and can only be cured by the blood of a noblewoman of royal blood. We do not know who the

lady is. Whenever a young maiden passes by, we seize her, for she may be the one to cure our mistress."

Balin looked at his companion. She agreed to give some of her blood to the knights, but it did not cure their mistress. The knights thanked them and requested that they rest at the castle until morning.

For the next few days, Balin and the lady searched for Garlon. They continued on in peace. On the third day, they arrived at a fine manor house. Seeing that the maiden needed rest, Balin led their horses to the manor. The lord of the manor welcomed them and offered them dinner and shelter for the night.

The lord told Balin about his son, who had been seriously wounded. During the course of the meal, the son frequently groaned and cried out in pain. Balin asked what had caused the son's injuries.

"He received a grievous wound by a

sword, but no hand held that sword and no knight appeared to claim the deed," the lord said. "I have consulted many wise men. They told me that the only cure for my son's wounds is the invisible knight's own blood."

"Perhaps I can help you," Balin said. "The knight who committed that crime is Sir Garlon. He has dishonored the noble calling of knighthood. We have been searching for this knight to avenge the wrongs that he has done. If you suggest a direction for our search, we will gladly continue until we find Sir Garlon."

"King Pellam has proclaimed a feast and invited all of the nobles and knights in this area. It is certain that this knight will attend. If you stay here until the feast day, I will ride with you to King Pellam's castle," the lord said.

On the appointed day, Balin went with the lady and the lord to Pellam's castle. They were cordially received and

taken to the banquet hall. Balin was careful to keep his sword concealed. As the festivities began, the lords and ladies talked freely. Balin turned and asked a nobleman sitting next to him to point out Sir Garlon.

Garlon was seated across from Balin. Now that the invisible knight could be seen, Balin judged him to be haughty and indiscreet. Garlon must have seen Balin scowling, for he came over and slapped Balin's face.

Balin was outraged and could not control his anger. He drew his sword and cut down Garlon in one stroke. He took some of the invisible knight's blood to cure the lord's son. Then he prepared to leave King Pellam's castle.

The king's knights stopped them. Pellam went up to Balin and said, "You will pay for murdering my brother and abusing my hospitality." The king took his sword and gave Balin a terrible blow. Balin raised his sword to fend off the blow, but the sword shattered. Without a weapon, Balin knew he would surely be defeated. So he ran through the castle, hoping to find a sword or a spear.

In a dimly lit, sumptuous room, he found a magnificent, intricately wrought spear. It lay on a table of pure gold, which was held up by four silver pillars. Balin picked up the spear just as King Pellam entered the room. Balin struck him, and the king fell.

The spear that Balin used to strike

the king was none other than the spear that had pierced Christ's body as he hung on the cross. Joseph of Arimathea had brought it to Britain, along with the Holy Grail. King Pellam was Joseph's descendant.

As Merlin had foretold, Balin had with one stroke changed the course of history. Pellam's castle came crashing down. Everyone in Pellam's court died. Three surrounding kingdoms became wastelands. And the wound that Balin

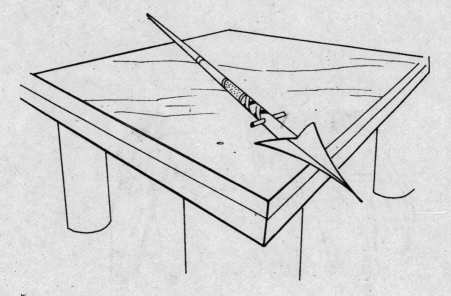

had given Pellam would remain open for many years.

Only King Pellam and Balin remained alive, but both were senseless. Merlin came to the castle and explained everything that had happened. Balin said farewell to Merlin and went on the last leg of his journey. Merlin's prophecy had been fulfilled, but the maiden from whom Balin took the sword had made another prophecy. Her prediction had not troubled Balin at the time, and now

he had forgotten it.

Eventually Balin came to a cross inscribed with these words:

ALL KNIGHTS BEWARE.
NONE MAY RIDE ALONE
TO THIS CASTLE.

Balin disregarded the warning and rode on until he saw an old man. The man raised an arm to stop him. "Heed the warning and turn back," the old man cried. Hearing a horn ring out in the distance, Balin ignored the man and urged his horse forward.

At the castle, Balin found many knights and fine ladies who encouraged him to join their amusements. After a while, the mistress of the castle came to Balin and invited him to joust with a knight who kept watch over an island. "You may not pass through here unless you defeat him," she said.

Balin did not want to fight anymore,

but he did not want to remain at the castle. While he prepared for battle, another knight offered him a shield. The shield was larger than Balin's. He accepted it gratefully. There were no markings on the shield to identify him, but Balin thought that it was unlikely that anyone at the castle would know him.

When he was ready to joust, Balin was escorted to the field. The knight of the island wore red armor. His horse

had a red harness. Balin was curious about the knight's identity, but the red knight had no markings on his shield, either.

The knights matched each other, blow for blow. After hours of fighting, neither one had gained the advantage. They were seriously wounded. Gasping for breath, Balin asked the red knight his name.

"Sir Balan, a knight of King Arthur's court," the red knight said.

Balin cried out in despair. "I have killed my own brother," he raved.

"And I have killed my own brother," Balan echoed him. "Do not despair, dear brother. I fought with the knight of the island. When I defeated him, I had to take his place. You might have reached this castle first and defeated the knight of the island. But the end of our stories would have been the same."

Knights from the castle buried the brothers in the same grave. Merlin came and took Balin's sword. He made a new handle for it and put it into the scabbard. Holding it out before him, he asked a knight to draw it from the scabbard. The knight could not do so. Merlin proclaimed that the sword was enchanted and could only be removed by a special knight.

Merlin built an enchanted bridge from the island to the mainland. Only knights of purity would be able to cross it. Using his magic, Merlin put the sword

into a marble block that sat in the water surrounding the island. The blade was visible above the water's surface and shone brilliantly. The scabbard was left on the land. Merlin predicted that one day, the most pure and noble knight would discover both and use them on his quest for the Holy Grail.

CHAPTER 4
ARTHUR MARRIES

Governing Britain kept Arthur very busy. He established his capital at Camelot, and brave knights from throughout the country came to serve him. Many said that during good King Arthur's reign, Britain would become peaceful and prosperous.

Looking at Camelot, one could see that this was so. Flower-filled meadows, fountains, and lush greenery provided the backdrop for lively court life. Birds of every color flitted through the trees, and noblemen and women dressed in fine clothing strolled along the well-kept lawns and pathways.

Arthur was devoted to his knights

and his subjects and had little time to think about his own needs. Still, when he had a few moments to himself, his thoughts turned to Guinevere, the daughter of King Leodegrance.

As was his custom when making any decisions that would affect the realm, Arthur consulted Merlin. The wizard looked gravely at the king, for he knew that a marriage with Guinevere would bring shame to the court. Yes, Guinevere had fallen in love with Arthur, but she

was destined to fall more deeply in love with another knight.

But Arthur wanted Guinevere and was determined to marry her. He asked Merlin to go to Leodegrance's castle at Cameliard and announce his intentions. Merlin did so, to Leodegrance's delight.

As a wedding gift, Leodegrance sent Arthur the Round Table, which had been given to him by Arthur's father, Uther Pendragon. One hundred and fifty knights could be seated at the table, but Leodegrance had only one hundred to send to Arthur with his gift. The others had been killed or captured.

While Arthur prepared for his grand wedding, Merlin was sent to find fifty knights to fill the empty seats, or sieges. Merlin returned with twenty-eight men worthy of sitting at the Round Table. Over the course of Arthur's reign, other worthy knights would prove themselves in battle and take their places at the table. When all one hundred and fifty were filled, then the knights would be called to the noblest challenge they would ever face and only one would be found worthy to achieve it.

The Archbishop of Canterbury came to bless the seats, and then the knights took their places. When they rose, their names were written in gold letters on the sieges. On one siege were the words "Siege Perilous," and next to that seat were two seats with no names on them.

Arthur was so happy that Guinevere was to be his wife. He proclaimed that any man who asked for a gift would be granted his wish on the wedding day, as long as it was a reasonable request.

Gawain, son of King Lot and Igraine's sister Margawse, came to ask Arthur to make him a knight. Arthur was pleased to do as his cousin asked, and he happily agreed to grant the wish on Gawain's wedding day.

Next came a poor cowherd to ask for a gift of the king. This man brought his

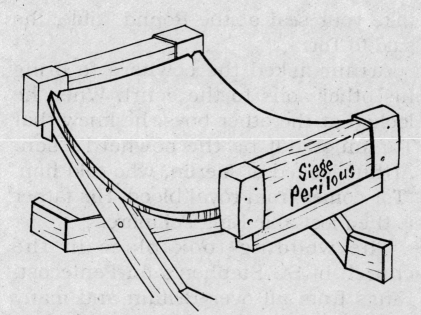

son and requested that Arthur make a knight of the boy. The cowherd explained that he had thirteen sons. All but this boy, called Tor, agreed to work in the fields and tend the animals. Tor thought only of battles and glory.

"Do you have a sword?" Arthur asked.

The boy showed Arthur his sword. Arthur took the sword, motioned for the boy to kneel, and touched his neck with the blade. "I will make you a knight. May you live to prove your worth and take your seat at the Round Table," he said to Tor.

Arthur asked the cowherd to bring his other sons to the court. When he looked at the other boys, he knew that Tor must not be the cowherd's son. Arthur looked at Merlin, who told him, "Tor comes from royal blood. His father is the most able King Pellinore."

The wedding took place in the church of St. Stephen's on Pentecost. Kings from all over Britain and many other countries attended, including King Pellinore. After the ceremony, there was a feast at which Arthur knighted Tor and Gawain. Looking at the Round Table, Arthur asked Merlin, "Why are those two seats empty and no names inscribed on them?"

Merlin explained that the names of the knights who would sit in those sieges would be revealed when they arrived to claim their places. As for the siege with the words, "Siege Perilous,"

only one man was destined to sit there. Anyone to sit there other than that man was doomed.

Then Merlin took King Pellinore by the hand and led him to a seat next to one of the empty seats. Gawain turned pale and looked at his brother, Gaheris. Both men hated Pellinore for killing their father, King Lot. But Arthur's hatred for Pellinore gave way to a greater appreciation of Merlin's vision. The wizard's words had once again been true: now Pellinore was a knight of the Round Table.

CHAPTER 5
LANCELOT FALLS FROM GRACE

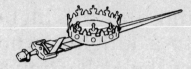

King Arthur was blessed to have the strongest and most courageous knights in his service. These knights were eager to prove themselves in battle and happily volunteered to defend any man or woman who was in danger from errant knights, thieves, or monstrous creatures. Whenever they set out on an adventure, the knights were sure to meet with villains who were jealous of their noble king and wanted revenge.

Of all of the illustrious knights that served King Arthur, Lancelot was ranked far above the others. This knight's feats astounded his peers and won the love and admiration of King Arthur and

Queen Guinevere. In the king's eyes, Lancelot could do no wrong.

But Lancelot's love of rewards and his unlawful love of Guinevere stood between him and the highest honor accorded to a knight: beholding the mysteries of the Holy Grail. Lancelot's attachment to fame and glory would be his undoing, but his failings would also produce one who could truly call himself a holy knight.

One day when the king and his knights were sitting down to a feast, a hermit came to them. Looking around the table, the hermit fixed his gaze on the empty seat, the Siege Perilous. He asked the king why the seat was vacant.

"It is said that the Siege Perilous is reserved for one man only. Any other man who tries to sit in this seat is in danger of losing his life," Arthur told the hermit.

"Indeed," the hermit replied, "this is true. And the one who is destined to sit

in the Siege Perilous will soon be born. The man who will father this holy child is a great knight, but his son will be greater still. By the child's virtue, he will achieve the Holy Grail."

Lancelot was stirred by the hermit's words. He left the castle in search of adventures that would prove that he was the greatest knight in the king's service. He had not ridden very far when he came to the city of Corbin. A small group of townspeople called for his aid. They

told him that there was a lady held prisoner in a castle tower close by. This lady was being tortured because two wicked queens were jealous of her beauty. One of the queens was the very powerful sorceress Morgan le Fay, half-sister to King Arthur.

The townspeople led Lancelot to the castle tower. He climbed up to the lady's chamber and found her in a room filled with steam. The wicked queens had arranged for the woman to be scalded by boiling water. They had decreed that only

the best knight could save her!

Lancelot escorted the lady from the chamber and outside the tower. She expressed her gratitude and begged Lancelot to accompany her to a chapel, where she could give thanks for her release. After they had prayed at the chapel, Lancelot and the lady were addressed by a group of villagers who lived near the chapel.

"Please save us from the serpent. The horrible creature lives in a tomb near our village. It has killed many of our people," they cried.

Lancelot agreed to help them. When he stood in front of the tomb, he read the inscription that was written in gold letters on the stone covering:

WHEN A LEOPARD OF ROYAL
BLOOD COMES, THE
SERPENT WILL BE SLAIN.
THIS LEOPARD'S SON WILL
ACHIEVE AN HONOR FOR
WHICH NO OTHER KNIGHT
ON EARTH IS WORTHY.

Then the tomb opened, and the fire-breathing serpent came out to meet Lancelot's challenge. Although the battle was long and hard, Lancelot defeated the serpent. The villagers gave a shout of joy and embraced their savior.

"What brave knight is this?" a voice rang out as a knight walked through

the crowd toward Lancelot.

"I am Sir Lancelot, a knight of King Arthur's court," Lancelot replied.

The knight was, in fact, King Pelles.

"I am a descendant of Joseph of Arimathea, who brought the Holy Grail to Britain. Now I am king over this territory and the guardian of the grail. Please join me at my castle. You have earned a fine meal and some rest."

King Pelles took Lancelot to his castle and led him to a banquet hall. After Lancelot had taken a seat, a dove flew through a window. It carried in its beak a small perfume bottle, from which rose the fragrance of frankincense and myrrh. As the dove flew over the table, a feast appeared on it, made up of fine foods and wine. A beautiful maiden came in. She held a golden vessel, before which the king knelt and prayed.

"This," said the king, "is the Holy Grail, and she is the Grail Maiden. This vessel is the greatest treasure, come down from heaven. Its mysteries will be revealed to the pure in heart. When it passes before the Knights of the Round Table, all one hundred and fifty of these noble servants will go out in search of the grail's mysteries."

After dinner, Lancelot was shown to a bedchamber. He was so tired that he barely noticed his surroundings. He fell into a deep sleep, dreaming of Queen Guinevere. He knew that she would

esteem him more highly now that he had slain the serpent and had seen the grail.

The next day, a knight from Arthur's court came to tell Lancelot that Queen Guinevere wished to see him. The knight said that the queen had gone to a castle not far from the Grail Castle. Lancelot was eager to see Guinevere and tell her about his great adventures. When they arrived, Lancelot was shown to a chamber where Guinevere welcomed him warmly.

At King Arthur's court, Guinevere and
Lancelot had to be very careful because
there were knights who had noticed
their love for each other. These knights
tried to find ways to dishonor the king
by revealing Guinevere's treachery. So
now that they were far from the court,
Lancelot let down his guard.

Early the next morning when Lancelot
rose from the bed, he thought he was
dreaming again. Instead of Guinevere, a
different beautiful woman was sleeping

peacefully beside him. When he realized that he was not dreaming, he was furious. His anguished cry woke the woman. Lancelot lifted his sword against her, but she pleaded for mercy.

"I am Elaine. King Pelles's daughter," she said. "Last night, we made a child. He is destined to be the purest knight, the only one who will be able to achieve the Holy Grail."

Lancelot forgave Elaine and quickly left the castle, but he was disturbed by

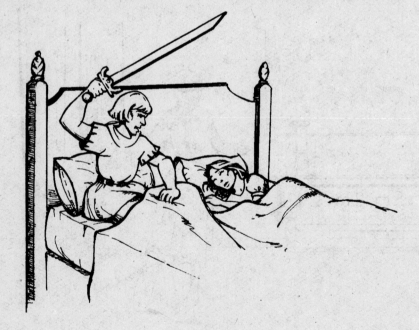

the trickery. He knew that Queen Guinevere would be angry if she learned that he had a son by another woman.

Elaine named the child Galahad. Soon after his birth, the news traveled throughout the country. Eventually, Guinevere heard that Lancelot had fathered the child. She summoned Lancelot and accused him of treachery. He explained to her that he had been deceived himself, but her pride had been wounded. She banished him from

her sight and told him never to approach her again.

Heartbroken, Lancelot fled the castle. His mind was so disordered that he did not care which road he traveled. For a number of years, he lived like a madman in the wild.

CHAPTER 6
THE KNIGHTS SEARCH FOR LANCELOT

In time, Guinevere's wrath had cooled and she wanted Lancelot back at the court. She asked three trusted knights who championed Lancelot to search for him. These knights were Sir Bors, Sir Ector and Sir Lionel.

After a few months of searching, Bors, Ector and Lionel met Sir Melion, who was on his way to Camelot. The knights asked Melion to tell King Arthur that they had failed to find Lancelot.

Arthur was disappointed by the news. He had been sure that Lancelot would come back because of his devotion to the court. Many other knights agreed to join the search, including Arthur's nephew

Gawain and brothers Aglovale and Percival. Their father was King Pellinore, and Sir Tor was their half-brother.

The knights rode off in pairs and had many dangerous adventures during their search. Sir Percival, in particular, proved to be a fierce knight and overcame many wicked opponents. One day, he met a knight whose spear and helmet were broken. Even though his weapons were damaged, the knight challenged Percival and they began to joust.

Percival was thrown from his horse, but would not give up. He motioned for the other knight to dismount and fight on the ground. Hours later, the two knights were still battling. Marveling at his opponent's strength, Percival raised his hand to speak.

"What great knight is this?" he asked, for he was amazed at the knight's great strength.

Percival was more amazed when he discovered that it was Sir Ector, who had ridden out with him to seek Lancelot. They were both seriously wounded. Each felt that he would die. Together they prayed and were given a vision of the Holy Grail. Faint though it was, Percival could see the Grail Maiden in the misty vision. He and Ector were healed of their wounds. Overjoyed, they left to continue their search for Lancelot.

Lancelot's trail was hard to find. The once-great knight was a half-starved wild man. In this state he arrived once again

at the city of Corbin, but he did not recognize it as the place where he had met King Pelles and Elaine. The townspeople were afraid of him, and the children taunted him. He continued walking until he came to the castle. Servants there gave him some food and straw to sleep on. Lancelot put the straw by the castle gate and made it his home.

At the same time, King Pelles was preparing to knight his nephew, Castor. The young man was in a jovial mood,

as he was now about to be given his heart's desire—knighthood. While he dressed, he thought that he had more than enough clothing and should disperse some of it to those in need. He gave Lancelot a scarlet robe, which transformed the beggar into a gentleman.

Wearing his new gown, Lancelot wandered back outside the castle. His outward appearance had changed, but he still felt and acted like a wounded beast. His pain pursued him like a relentless enemy. Exhausted, he lay down by a well to sleep.

Elaine and her maids were enjoying the fine weather in the garden. One of the maids recognized Lancelot and pointed him out to her mistress. Elaine rose and went to see her father. He had Lancelot carried to the tower in which the grail was kept. At the king's command, a monk unveiled the grail. Instantly, Lancelot was healed of his wounds. His mind became peaceful. But because of his trespasses he had not been granted a vision of the grail's mysteries.

Now that Lancelot's mind was restored, the shame that he had brought on King Arthur and his court horrified him. Lancelot told King Pelles that he could not return there. Lancelot asked King Pelles for a castle in which he could live out the rest of his days.

The king agreed to Lancelot's request. Along with many knights and servants, the king rode with Lancelot, Elaine and their son, Galahad, to the Castle of Bliant, which was built on an island. When Lancelot saw the beautiful lake surrounding the castle, he called his new home Joyous Island.

Lancelot tried to adjust to his new life, which was quiet and peaceful, but he longed for knightly adventures. When he heard that a tournament was to be held at a castle close by, he felt that nothing could keep him away. He sent a servant

to the castle to announce that "the knight who lives in shame" welcomed all challengers. If any knight could defeat Lancelot, the victor would be rewarded with a beautiful maiden and a falcon.

The tournament drew five hundred knights, but none could beat Lancelot. And none was killed in battle. Victor and vanquished rejoiced when the jousting was done. Lancelot was so happy that he held a feast in honor of his opponents.

As chance or fate would have it, Sir

Percival and Sir Ector, who were still searching for Lancelot, arrived at the shore of the lake. Seeing the castle, they wanted to cross the lake and ask if any there had seen Lancelot. Since they had no way to cross the lake, they remained on the shore until a maiden appeared on the opposite side.

"Dear lady, who lives in the castle?" Percival asked.

The maiden told them about the knight who lived there and his strange

history. She advised them to walk along the shore and soon they would come to a boat. In it, they could travel to the island and meet the knight.

Percival wanted to joust with the knight, so he asked Ector to remain on the shore and wait until he was finished. It would not be fair, he said, to challenge the knight of the island with another knight by his side. Then Percival walked until he found the boat, rowed to the island, and went to the castle.

"I wish to joust with the knight who lives here," Percival said to the porter.

The porter went off to relay Percival's challenge to his master and returned with a company of fine gentlemen and ladies from Lancelot's court. Soon Lancelot rode into the open and met Percival's challenge.

After more than two hours of fighting, both knights were wounded and had very little strength left. Percival raised his head and asked, "Most worthy

knight, will you tell me your name?"

"I am the knight who lives in shame," Lancelot replied. "Which worthy knight have I jousted with this day?"

"Percival, son of King Pellinore and knight of noble King Arthur's court," Percival said.

When Lancelot heard this, he hung his head and said, "I am Sir Lancelot, son of King Ban, formerly a knight of King Arthur's court."

The two knights embraced, and Sir Ector was brought to the island. Percival and Ector begged Lancelot to return to the court. So many years had passed, and Lancelot still felt that his shame deprived him of a place at King Arthur's court. Percival assured him that the king and queen had spared no expense in searching for Lancelot. They had forgiven him. They only wanted their best knight to return to their service.

Lancelot's heart mended when he heard these words. Elaine knew that nothing she could do would keep Lancelot on Joyous Island. She loved him and wanted him to be happy, so she let him go. She asked that Lancelot honor her wish that Galahad, who now was fifteen years old, be knighted when Pentecost arrived.

PART III
THE HOLY GRAIL

CHAPTER 1
GALAHAD TAKES HIS SEAT

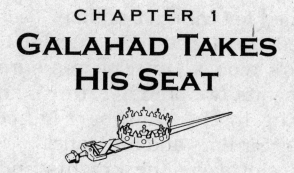

Every year since his coronation, King Arthur had held a great feast on Pentecost. So this year when Pentecost arrived, the king and his knights, as usual, assembled at the Round Table to celebrate. They rejoiced to have Lancelot with them after so long a separation.

Just as the feast began, a fine lady came before the king with a request for Lancelot. She said that she had come from the castle of King Pelles and wanted Lancelot to accompany her into the forest. Lancelot agreed to go. With Arthur's consent, they left Camelot right away on horseback.

When they reached an abbey, the lady

motioned for Lancelot to stop. The nuns greeted them and led Lancelot to the abbess's rooms. Lancelot was surprised to recognize two of King Arthur's knights sleeping in the chamber: Lancelot's cousins Sir Bors and Sir Lionel.

Lancelot woke the knights and told them about the lady who had brought him there. As he spoke, twelve nuns came into the chamber with a young man. Again, Lancelot was surprised, for the youth was his son, Galahad.

One of the nuns told Lancelot that Galahad had been given into their care. Now he was ready to be knighted, she said, and she asked Lancelot to do so.

Lancelot turned to Galahad. "Is this your wish?" he asked his son. Galahad assented. The next morning, before Lancelot and his cousins left the abbey, he knighted Galahad.

"Will you return to Camelot with us?" Lancelot asked Galahad.

"I will join you there, Father," Galahad

replied, "but it is not time yet."

So Lancelot and his companions left the abbey, overjoyed that soon Arthur's court would receive such a fine and noble youth.

They arrived at the king's castle in time to sit down for dinner with the king and the other knights. The whole company was astonished to see that a

new inscription had appeared on the empty siege. It said:

ON THIS DAY, THE MOST
PURE AND WORTHY KNIGHT
SHALL TAKE HIS PLACE IN
THIS SEAT.

The knights started talking among themselves about what this could mean for the Round Table, but Arthur called for a covering to be placed over

the seat. He knew that when the time came, the knight would appear to claim his place.

Just as the knights had settled down, their curiosity was aroused once again. A squire had come in to announce that a stone was floating in the river outside the castle. A mighty sword was lodged in the stone.

Arthur led his knights to the river. Just as the squire described, there was an object floating in the water. It was a block of red marble. The sword's hilt protruded from the block. Gold letters shined brightly from the hilt in the soft twilight. Arthur drew near to read the inscription. It read:

FALSE KNIGHTS BEWARE.
NO MAN SHALL TAKE THIS
SWORD EXCEPT THE MAN FOR
WHOM IT IS DESTINED. THIS
KNIGHT SHALL BE THE BEST
KNIGHT ON EARTH.

Arthur asked Lancelot to try to draw the sword out of the stone.

"Sire," Lancelot replied, "I am not the best knight on earth."

Then Arthur asked his nephew, Gawain, to try, but Gawain did not want to. Arthur ordered him to try, but Gawain could not draw the sword.

Next, Arthur turned to Percival and commanded the reluctant knight to try his hand on the sword. But Percival could not remove it from the block of marble, either. Finally, Arthur agreed to return to dinner and leave the sword.

By this time, no one was hungry, but all were eager for an explanation of the strange events they had witnessed. They did not have long to wait, because after they were served, the light in the hall dimmed and an eerie silence descended over the court.

An old hermit dressed in a white robe walked slowly into the hall. He was

accompanied by a knight in red armor. An intricate scabbard hung at the knight's side, but he did not have a sword or a shield.

"Sire, this knight is the pure and noble knight who will complete your great company," the hermit proclaimed. Arthur nodded solemnly.

The hermit motioned for the red knight to remove the armor. The old man led the red knight to the Siege Perilous. He removed the cover that Arthur had placed over the inscription and motioned for the red knight to sit down. The king and the other knights gasped when they saw the letters. They had rearranged themselves and now read:

THIS SIEGE SHALL NOW
BE FILLED BY THE NOBLE
KNIGHT, SIR GALAHAD.

When Galahad finally took his seat, the company stared in silence for a while. "This is the knight that will achieve the Holy Grail," one whispered to another. Arthur looked reverently at the new member of the Round Table. He noticed the look of joy on Lancelot's face. For once, the most troubled knight of the Round Table was at peace.

King Arthur requested that Galahad come with him to the river. When they arrived, he asked Galahad to try to draw the sword out of the marble block. Galahad easily drew the sword

from the marble and placed it in his scabbard.

"Sir, this sword was destined for my hand," he told Arthur. "It belonged to Sir Balin, the knight who fought and killed his brother, Balan. Balin gave my great-grandfather, King Pellam, a wound that only I can heal."

To honor the new knight, the king called for a tournament. He wanted to see if Galahad's powers were, indeed, above that of all the other knights at the court. Galahad's courage and endurance were proven beyond any doubt. The only knights he could not defeat were his father, Lancelot, and Percival.

At the end of the jousting, everyone rejoiced and congratulated Galahad. But King Arthur was solemn. He knew that Galahad's appearance at the court signaled a great change. Soon his knights would ride out on a quest that would dissolve the Round Table.

CHAPTER 2
A Vision and a Quest

The exhausted knights said evening prayer and went to the banquet hall for dinner. Surely, they thought, they had seen enough wonders for one day. They did not know that within a few minutes, they would be given a vision of the Holy Grail.

The grail procession began with a clap of thunder and a blinding light. Then the room was shrouded in darkness. A golden vessel, covered with pure white silk, hovered above the ground, as if held by an invisible hand. The scent of frankincense and myrrh rose from the vessel and filled the room. When the knights looked down, they saw that the table now

was filled with their favorite foods. When they looked up, the grail had vanished.

Gawain was the first to speak. "Sire, we have been granted this feast and give thanks. But none of us has seen the Holy Grail, for it was covered. Please grant that I may leave this court in search of the holy vessel."

Many of the other knights requested that they be allowed to search for the Holy Grail, as well. Arthur knew that he could not dissuade them, but he

was sad that this fine company of men would never again sit together at the Round Table. He understood that many would die in the effort, and others would be wounded.

The next day, the one hundred and fifty Knights of the Round Table left Camelot. All of them would have grand adventures in their search, but few would witness miracles and see wonders.

Galahad rode for some time before he met with any unusual circumstances.

One day, though, he came to an abbey where the monks called him to stop. They took him to a chamber in which he found two of Arthur's knights, Bagdemagus and Uwayne. They told Galahad that they had come to the abbey in search of a miraculous shield. It was said that taking the shield would put a knight in great danger.

Bagdemagus said that he intended to take the shield. He asked Galahad to bear the shield if he failed to achieve the adventure on which the shield would lead him. Since Galahad did not have a shield, he agreed.

In the morning, a monk gave Bagdemagus the shield. It was white with a red cross marking the center. Then, taking a squire with him, Bagdemagus rode off.

An hour later the two reached a hermitage. A knight in white armor on a white horse approached them with his spear raised. The white knight unhorsed

Bagdemagus and took his shield.

"This shield does not belong to you," the white knight said. "It belongs to Sir Galahad. You must give it to him."

So, with the help of his squire, Bagdemagus returned to the abbey and gave Galahad the shield. Bagdemagus remained at the abbey to heal from his wounds, but Galahad rode off. He wanted to find the white knight and ask him about the shield. Galahad had no trouble finding the hermitage and the white knight, who was willing to tell him about the shield.

"This shield was made in the Holy Land," the knight said. "Joseph of Arimathea brought it to Britain, along with the Holy Grail and the spear that

pierced Christ's body as it hung on the cross. When Joseph was dying, he marked the shield with a cross, using his own blood. The shield has been in this abbey for safekeeping. Now it is yours to take."

Galahad knew that the shield was part of his destiny. The white knight's task was done, and he vanished. Awed by what he had witnessed, the squire wanted to travel with Galahad on his quest. The squire requested that Galahad make him a knight.

When Galahad learned that the squire was the king of Denmark's son, he agreed to make him a knight the following morning. Together the new knight, called Sir Melias, rode off with Galahad to search for the Holy Grail.

CHAPTER 3
A PARTING
OF THE WAYS

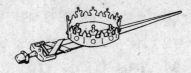

G alahad and Melias rode for days without any adventures. Then they came to a crossroads marked by a sign that read:

HE WHO TAKES THE ROAD
TO THE RIGHT TAKES THE
EASY ROAD. HE WHO
CHOOSES THE ROAD TO THE
LEFT MUST PROVE HIS WORTH.

Melias asked that Galahad allow him to take the road to the left. Although Galahad knew that Melias would not fare well on the hard road, he granted Melias's wish.

Melias's road took him through the forest. After two days, he arrived at a meadow. A dwelling drew his attention. When he looked through the window, he saw a golden crown sitting on a chair. Next to the chair was a table set for a feast. Melias took the crown and rode away. After a few minutes, he heard someone shouting.

"Come back, thief! The crown does not belong to you," the voice cried. It belonged to a knight, who rode up to

Melias and challenged him to a joust. The knight swiftly unhorsed Melias and rode away with the crown.

Melias was badly wounded but relieved when, not long after, Galahad rode by. He took Melias to an abbey and asked the monks to care for the wounded knight. Poor Melias was wounded in spirit as well as in his body. He knew that his pride had caused his downfall.

Galahad stayed with Melias at the abbey for a few days. When he left, he did not know in which direction he should go. After traveling for many days, Galahad saw a chapel that was hidden away on a mountainside. The chapel had long been deserted, but Galahad wanted to say a prayer.

After Galahad said his prayer, a voice rose up as if in answer. The voice told him to travel to a castle in the Severn Valley and free its inhabitants. So Galahad took his weapons and went to the castle. Along the way, he was warned about the terrible knights at the castle who had enslaved the people, but Galahad would not turn back.

When he arrived at the castle, seven knights came out to meet him. "This is the Maidens' Castle, and we are its keepers. If you fight us, you will meet your end," one of the knights said.

Galahad would not turn away, so the knights came forward. Although he was outnumbered, it did not take long for Galahad to defeat the wicked knights. They fled, leaving him free to walk through the castle.

A lady in the castle told Galahad that the knights were sure to return. She said that Galahad must blow on an ivory horn, which she gave him. "Upon hearing the sound of this horn, all of the knights under this castle's rule will come. You must demand that the knights swear allegiance to the rightful ruler of these lands."

Galahad agreed and blew on the horn. He turned to ask the lady about the rightful ruler, but she was gone. A priest walked by, so Galahad asked him.

"Seven years ago, seven brothers came to this castle and murdered the duke," the priest explained. "The group tortured his daughter, and she died soon after their arrival. Before she died, she foretold that a brave and noble knight would release the castle from the evil brothers' tyranny. Since then, the wicked brothers have killed every knight who has passed through this land."

By this time, all of the knights under the brothers' rule had arrived. Galahad persuaded them to swear allegiance to the duke's youngest daughter, who was still alive. The captives in the castle rejoiced at this news, but then Galahad remembered that the lady had predicted the brothers' return.

The evening passed with peace, though, and in the morning a messenger arrived with great news. Three of Arthur's knights had killed the wicked knights. When Galahad heard that the knights were Gawain, Gareth and Uwayne, he left to follow them. Perhaps, he thought, he could join them in some other adventure.

CHAPTER 4
IN SEARCH
OF GALAHAD

Gawain had heard about Galahad's shield from Melias. After he left Camelot, Gawain found the abbey where the shield was kept. Melias still was recovering from his grievous wounds, but he was well enough to tell Gawain his story.

The tale whet Gawain's appetite for excitement. He decided to look for Galahad in the hopes of sharing some adventures. Before he left, Sir Gareth passed by the abbey. Together they rode off in search of Galahad.

On the road they met Sir Uwayne. "Tell us, what grand adventures have you found?" Gawain asked. Uwayne had not found any.

"Gawain and I were just lamenting our lack of opportunity to save a lady or joust with a knight," Gareth said.

The three knights continued together and, before too long, entered the Severn Valley. The seven brothers from the Maidens' Castle observed them and decided to avenge themselves on the unsuspecting knights.

The brothers were, indeed, wicked, but they could not match Arthur's

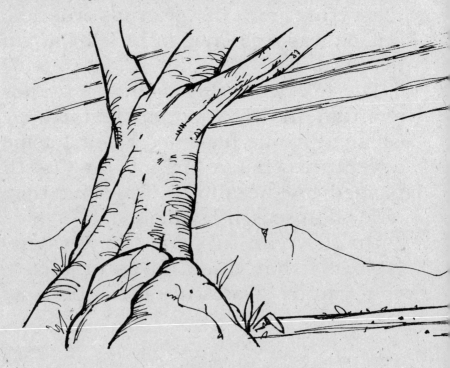

knights. Soon, the brothers lay on the ground, never to rise again. Gawain led his companions to the castle, where they heard the rest of the story. Since Galahad had left the Maidens' Castle, Gawain suggested that the three knights might find him sooner if they went in different directions.

Meanwhile, Galahad's path took him to the Waste Land, a desolate area that surrounded King Pelles's castle. Seeing two knights exploring, he rode up to

them and challenged them to a joust. It was Lancelot and Percival. Because he had an unfamiliar device on his shield, they did not recognize Galahad.

Galahad's mastery astounded the two knights. After he had unhorsed both of them, Galahad rode off. An anchorite living in a hermitage nearby witnessed the joust. She called to Galahad by name as he rode past.

"How do you know me?" Galahad asked her.

"You are the blessed Galahad, the one true knight on earth," she said.

Galahad did not want Lancelot and Percival to know who had beaten them, so he left quickly. But they had seen him talking to the anchorite. Percival wanted to question her, but Lancelot decided to go in another direction.

Lancelot went off into the forest, and Percival rode to the anchorite. He said that he wanted to find the knight with the cross on his shield and asked her if

she knew his identity.

"If it is revenge you seek," she said to Percival, "seek no more. The knight who defeated you and your companion is not your enemy. He is Sir Galahad, the noble and true knight who will achieve the Holy Grail. If you choose to follow him on his quest, go to the Grail Castle. Surely, you will find news of him there." Percival thanked the anchorite and left.

Meanwhile, Lancelot had come to a crossroads, which was marked by a stone cross. Light streaming from the window of a chapel close by caught his eye. He walked over to the chapel. Through the window, he saw an altar. Six lighted candles in an ornate silver holder sat on a silver table. Lancelot had a strange desire to move toward the light. Finding a door in the side of the chapel, he tried to open it, but it would not budge.

Since night had already fallen, Lancelot decided to sleep by the chapel.

Perhaps in the morning, he thought, someone would come to open the chapel. He fell into a deep sleep, but woke when he heard horses' hooves rustling in the leaves.

A man led two horses into the clearing. Between them, they carried a piece of cloth stretched between two poles. It bore a knight, who moaned as if in great pain.

The knight prayed for healing. As he spoke, the table rose from the floor of the chapel and came through the door toward the stone cross. A vessel that was covered in white silk appeared before the wounded knight. He struggled up from the cloth and kneeled in front of the vessel. He was very weak, but managed to lift his chin and brush the vessel with his lips in a faint kiss. Instantly, he was healed of his wounds.

The table, the grail and the candlestick shimmered before him for a while, but then moved back into the chapel. The man who had led the horses helped the knight into his armor. The knight took Lancelot's horse, helmet and sword and rode away with his attendant.

Lancelot lay stunned on the ground. He could not move. He had seen how the Holy Grail had healed the wounded man. Although his body was whole, he felt in need of healing. He wanted the Holy Grail to come to him and heal his soul.

Since he didn't have his horse, he walked slowly and aimlessly away from the chapel. Seeing a hermitage in the distance, he decided to go there and ask the hermit to hear his confession. He told the holy man about his love for Arthur's wife, Queen Guinevere and how it prevented him from being healed by the grail. The hermit gave Lancelot a penance and asked him to stay at the hermitage.

CHAPTER 5
THE QUEST
CONTINUES

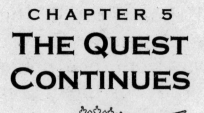

Arthur's knights were good servants of the kingdom, but only a few of them understood the true nature of their quest. Many of them believed that by fighting enemies in armed combat and saving maidens from thieves and murderers, they were performing their duties. During the time they searched for the grail, these knights had many adventures, but none were granted a vision of the holy vessel.

There were a few men of heart and courage whose noble characters took them further on the quest. These men were granted adventures that tested their inner strength and wisdom. They discovered that through their pride, jealousy and greed, they could be tempted away from their noble mission.

Some of the worthiest knights, like Percival, Lancelot, Gawain and Bors, were granted visions that revealed to these knights what stood between them and the Holy Grail. With the help of holy men, the visions were interpreted and the knights were told what they must do to overcome their weaknesses.

Lancelot and Gawain could not—or would not—conquer their weaknesses, but Percival and Bors remained steadfast. Of all one hundred and fifty Knights of the Round Table, only these two men were with Galahad when he achieved the Holy Grail.

After Percival and Bors had reflected on their visions, prayed, and confessed, they were taken away on an enchanted ship to wait for Galahad.

The one true knight had continued through the Waste Land. Along the way,

he found many opportunities to test his strength and save innocent people from injustices. Eventually Galahad rode by a castle. A tournament was being held there, so he decided to stop. When he saw that the knights of the castle needed help against their opponents, he joined the battle.

Some of Arthur's knights were fighting for the opponents. Gawain and Ector recognized Galahad and tried to stay clear of him. In the confusion, this proved to be impossible. Eventually, Galahad approached his fellows and gave Gawain a terrible wound with his mighty sword. Ector took Gawain into the castle, hoping that his friend could be healed.

As soon as Galahad was certain that the knights of the castle had gained the advantage, he left. Feeling tired, he decided to stop at a hermitage for the night. At this point, he was not far from the Grail Castle. The hermit welcomed

him and gave him a place to sleep.

Not long after he had fallen asleep, he was awakened by a knock on the door. The hermit came in with a noblewoman, who requested that Galahad accompany her to a castle by the sea. Galahad agreed, and they left the hermitage.

Soon Galahad and the noblewoman reached the castle by the sea. The mistress of the castle welcomed them. The noblewoman said that they would be grateful for a few hours of rest at the castle, but would leave before dawn.

Before they left, the mistress gave Galahad a new shield. Then the noblewoman took Galahad's hand and led him to the sea. In the waves, a ship was rocking peacefully. Galahad and the noblewoman boarded the ship. Percival and Bors, who were already on board, embraced Galahad.

"Tell me, my friends, what trials brought you here?" Galahad asked.

They told Galahad about their grand

adventures. "Indeed, you are worthy knights," Galahad said. "You have faced and defeated many temptations and are now ready to follow me on this journey."

As the ship glided through the sea, the knights rejoiced that they were together. "Our company would be complete if your father, Sir Lancelot, were among us," Bors said.

Galahad nodded his head but said, "That is not to be. This journey had been foretold and unravels according to a plan laid out before we were born. Although we cannot see the steps before we take them, we must continue with faith that we will achieve what we set out to find."

The knights looked across the sea and saw a second ship coming toward them. The noblewoman said that the first part of their journey was about to end. "You must consider whether you are ready for the next part."

Their vessel sailed easily through the

water and came up against the second ship. An inscription on the prow stood out clearly. It read:

NO MAN SHALL BOARD THIS
VESSEL, EXCEPT HE WHOSE
FAITH IS UNSHAKEABLE. IF YOU
ARE A TRUE KNIGHT, HAVE NO
FEAR. YOU WILL BE WELCOMED.

Galahad moved to board the ship, and the others followed. They silently walked

through the passages, marveling at the elaborate decorations. In one chamber, Galahad found a crown made of silk and a sword on a bed. The sword had been partially drawn from its sheath. The sword was a masterful work of art.

An inscription on the sword read:

THE HILT OF THIS SWORD
WAS CREATED FOR ONE HAND.
IT BELONGS TO A KNIGHT OF
SURPASSING VIRTUE.

Galahad felt his hand tingle. He knew that the sword was designed for him, but when Percival said that he would like to try, Galahad stepped aside.

Percival gripped the sword and tried with all of his strength to raise it from the bed. He could not lift it. He motioned for Bors to try. Bors failed, as well. After a few moments, Galahad walked to the bed, lightly gripped the sword, and gently raised it from the bed. Percival and Bors hung their heads. Once again, their pride had blinded them to the truth about themselves and their noble companion.

"Do not be sorrowful," Galahad said. "I will carry this sword for all of us. It will give us courage and strength for the final adventures on our quest for the Holy Grail."

CHAPTER 6
A TURN IN THE ROAD

When he left the hermitage, Lancelot was full of remorse. He vowed to dedicate himself to serving the king as a true knight. He promised to end his relationship with Queen Guinevere. Still, his road did not get easier. The more he thought of his failings, the more they troubled him. He realized that when his goal was to be the fiercest, most highly regarded knight, he was content. When he began to seek goodness and saw how far he had fallen, his shortcomings caused Lancelot great pain.

In time, he came to a valley and stopped by a river. The water swirled

and churned, just as Lancelot's mind did. Lancelot decided to cross the water and see where this new path took him.

On the other side, a knight in black armor approached him. Without any warning, the knight killed Lancelot's horse and rode off. Without a horse, Lancelot was forced to make the journey on foot. He sat near his weapons and sighed.

Weary from his trials, Lancelot soon fell asleep. As he dreamed, he heard a voice counsel him to take the next ship that came to the shore. When he woke, he was astonished to see a ship in the shallow water. He boarded it and let the waves direct his course.

Lancelot lived on the ship for weeks, with brief stops on land only when he needed food. One day, while he was walking along the shore looking for something to eat, a knight rode up to him. It was Galahad!

The young knight told his father about meeting Percival and Bors on the enchanted ship. Their journey, he said, had brought them to the coast of Scotland, where they were forced to defend themselves against some wicked knights. After defeating their enemies, Galahad said, his fellows agreed to part, hoping to meet again at the Grail Castle.

Being with his son gave Lancelot great happiness. For months, they lived together in peace. One day, though, a knight in white armor came for Galahad.

"It is time for you to leave this place and continue on your quest," the knight said.

Galahad went with the white knight, and Lancelot boarded his ship. He did not care where it took him. He doubted that he would ever be granted his heart's desire: to be healed by the Holy Grail.

One night, Lancelot noticed a castle off shore. He could not say why, but something inside told him to visit the castle. He moored his ship and went ashore, approaching the castle.

As he came closer, he saw the moon-light glinting off an open gate. Two lions stood watch by the gate. Lancelot drew his sword, preparing to fight the lions if necessary. A dwarf ran up to him and knocked the sword out of his hand.

"You will not need a sword here," the dwarf said. "It is a holy place."

Thanking the dwarf, Lancelot walked through the gate. The castle seemed to be deserted, but passing one door he heard sounds coming from inside. Someone was singing praises.

Lancelot prayed along with the voice, and the door opened. A brilliant stream of light blinded him.

When he recovered, he saw a silver table. A vessel covered with white cloth sat in the center of the table. Lancelot knew that, once again, he was in the presence of the Holy Grail.

Throughout his travels on this quest, wise and holy men had told Lancelot that he would not be granted a vision of the grail because of his pride and greed. He had done great deeds to impress King Arthur's queen and win acclaim rather than to help those in need. He knew that he was not worthy to behold its mysteries, but he could not stop himself.

With each step he took, he felt the heat in the room intensify. When he was a few feet from the table, he felt his

body consumed by flames. He was not in pain, but he could not see or hear anything. He tried to scream, but no sound came from his lips. He stumbled over something and hit the ground. Before he fainted, he felt arms lift him up and carry him out of the room.

The castle's servants tended Lancelot for the next twenty-four days. His heart beat, but in all other ways he was dead to the world. On the twenty-fifth day, he woke. He was agitated, so the servants called a priest.

Lancelot told the priest about the strange dreams he had had during his long sleep. The priest told him that the twenty-four days he was tormented by the dreams was his penance for twenty-four years of transgression.

When Lancelot heard that he was in the Grail Castle, he wept. He had come so close, but knew that he would not be granted a vision of the grail. But he also knew that his trials had changed him. His past life was gone. The remainder of his days on earth, he decided, must be spent in serving others.

The Grail Castle's keeper, King Pelles, welcomed Lancelot. Pelles had not seen Lancelot since the knight had left Joyous Island.

"My beautiful daughter, Elaine, is dead," Pelles said. "She loved you, Lancelot, and she was honored to give birth to the noble Galahad. When she died, she had no regrets."

Lancelot hung his head. "Thank you, sir, for this news. I must go now. I have come as far as I can on this quest. I must return to Camelot and see how the others have fared."

When Lancelot arrived at Camelot, he found that Gawain and a few other knights had come back. Arthur told Lancelot that most of the other knights had died or had been seriously wounded.

"I believe that only three knights are still on their quests," Lancelot said. "Percival, Bors, and my son, Galahad. Sire, pray that they will achieve what they seek and return whole to this castle."

CHAPTER 7
THE QUEST COMES TO AN END

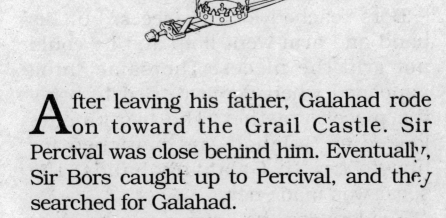

After leaving his father, Galahad rode on toward the Grail Castle. Sir Percival was close behind him. Eventually, Sir Bors caught up to Percival, and they searched for Galahad.

Percival and Bors rejoiced when they arrived at the Grail Castle and found that Galahad was, indeed, there. King Pelles took them to a chamber where Galahad was resting. Pelles welcomed them all and blessed them.

"You have been steadfast in your pursuit of virtue," the king said. "Soon, you will be rewarded."

King Pelles's son, Prince Eliazar, came into the chamber. He held a broken spear.

"Jospeh of Arimathea, the one who brought the grail to our country, was wounded with this spear," the prince said. "One of you must restore the spear to its original condition."

Bors reached for the pieces, but his hand and arm went limp and he could not grip the pieces. The same thing happened when Percival tried to bring the pieces together. The two knights looked at Galahad and motioned for him to try. In Galahad's hands, the spear was made new.

The king led the knights to a banquet hall for dinner. Noblemen and women from many countries entered the hall after them. After everyone was seated, four knights came in, carrying an old man on a bed. The man moaned.

"This is my father, King Pellam," Pelles said. "Years ago, he received an incurable wound from Sir Balin, which only the one true knight can heal."

The lights dimmed and the hall grew

silent. The door to the hall opened again. Maidens dressed in white carried candles. Then another maiden entered the hall. She held a spear. Blood dripped from its tip into a silver vessel, which she held beneath the spear. The Grail Maiden came in at the end of the procession. She held the holy vessel. It was still covered with a white cloth.

Galahad rose and walked toward the maiden holding the spear. He took the spear and went to King Pellam, touching his wound with the tip of the spear. The old man rose from the bed, kneeled before Galahad, and wept.

The Grail Maiden lifted her hand and gave a sign for Galahad to join her. When he stood in front of her, she held out the grail. Galahad removed its covering and beheld the vessel. He took a sip of the water it contained. Then he held the grail up for all to see. His quest was now accomplished.

The Grail Maiden led the procession

out of the hall. The banquet continued in silence. That evening, Galahad heard a voice telling him to take his two companions and leave the castle.

The knights rode night and day until they came to the sea. The enchanted ship was moored there, waiting to take Galahad away. Before he boarded the ship, he embraced Percival and Bors. He asked Bors to give his father a message.

"Give my father my blessing. Tell him to remember that this life will pass.

Earthly acclaim cannot equal virtue's rewards."

Percival and Bors remained on the shore until the ship passed out of sight. Percival decided not to return to Camelot. He turned his horse in the direction of an abbey, in which he hoped to spend his last days in prayer and fasting.

Bors traveled on alone. When he reached Camelot, the court was somber. So many knights had died in the quest. The news that Galahad had achieved it was received gratefully.

Arthur asked Bors and Lancelot to relate their stories so that all would know about the quest for the Holy Grail, and that a knight of the Round Table was the one to achieve it.

About the Author

During the 1400s, there were at least six Sir Thomas Malorys. Sir Thomas Malory of Newbold Revel, Warwickshire, is believed to be the true author of King Arthur and the Knights of the Round Table, because the life he led mimics the tales just read.

Sir Thomas Malory of Newbold Revel was born in the 1400s in Warwickshire, England. He became a knight for the Earl of Warwick and fought in the siege of Calais, France, in 1436. Mallory was captured and sent to prison. He made various attempts to escape, but never succeeded.

The knight-prisoner starting writing *Le Morte d'Arthur* in French, which, in later years, was translated in English to *The Knights of the Round Table.* Sir Thomas Malory died in 1471.

Treasury of Illustrated Classics

Adventures of Huckleberry Finn
The Adventures of Pinocchio
The Adventures of Robin Hood
The Adventures of Sherlock Holmes
The Adventures of Tom Sawyer
Alice in Wonderland
Anne of Green Gables
Beauty and the Beast
Black Beauty
The Call of the Wild
Frankenstein
Great Expectations
Gulliver's Travels
Heidi
Jane Eyre
Journey to the Center of the Earth
The Jungle Book
King Arthur and the Knights of the Round Table
The Legend of Sleepy Hollow & Rip Van Winkle
A Little Princess
Little Women
Moby Dick
Oliver Twist
Peter Pan
The Prince and the Pauper
Pygmalion
Rebecca of Sunnybrook Farm
Robinson Crusoe
The Secret Garden
Swiss Family Robinson
The Time Machine
Treasure Island
20,000 Leagues Under the Sea
White Fang
The Wind in the Willows
The Wizard of Oz